LOST ANGEL

By JANET FIELD HEATH

Illustrated by

JANET LAURA SCOTT

Brown Watson

ENGLAND

LONG AGO, on that first Christmas Eve, when the angels came out from Heaven to bring their tidings of great joy, there was a very little angel who slipped out with them. She was so little she did not sing very well, and, to tell the truth, she didn't quite understand what the angels were singing.

"*Glory to God in the highest, and on earth peace, good will toward men.*"—Yes, she knew about that, but what was it the beautiful big angel alone was singing?

"*For unto you is born this day, in the city of David, a Saviour.... Ye shall find the babe wrapped in swaddling clothes, lying in a manger.*"

The little angel didn't know what swaddling clothes were. And what—oh, what—was a manger?

Wondering, she floated down to the grassy fiel
below her to wait until the angels finished singin
and could take her back to Heaven. And in th
field, huddled close together, she found the shee
that the shepherds had forgotten. They were s
soft, so warm, so quiet that the little angel la
down among them and fell asleep.

When she woke up, it was very still. The big angels had gone back into Heaven, and the shepherds were hurrying to find the new baby about whom the angels had sung.

"I'm glad the big star is there," said the little angel. "But I wish the big angels had waited for me. I had better try and find them. I'm sure I can't find my way back to Heaven without them."

She straightened the crown upon her golden head and picked up her little harp which had fallen to one side. Then, gently spreading her wings, she went out onto the roadside.

"Why, there is one of the angels now," she cried and hurried to him.

But it wasn't an angel she found—only a man,

a man walking by himself, his head hung down so that he did not see even the great star.

The little angel looked at him. "Why don't you sing?" she asked.

"*Sing!* Why should I sing? What is there to sing about?" growled the man.

"It makes you happy to sing," laughed the
little angel. She ran her fingers across the harp she
was carrying and sang softly a little song. "There,
isn't that pretty?"

"Very, very pretty," said the man, looking at
her at last.

"Here, you take it—then you can sing," said
the little one, putting the harp into his hands. "And
please, will you tell me if the angels went this way?"

"Angels? Angels?"

"Didn't you see them?" asked the little one.
"Oh, see! Isn't that one of them just beyond us?"

She flew on to look, but alas, again it was a stranger to whom she came—a woman this time. Her clothes were rich and gay but her face was hard and sullen, and she spoke roughly to the little angel.

"Go away! Go away! I'm no fit person for a child to be seen with."

"Is it because you've lost your crown?" asked the angel anxiously. "Because, if you have, you may have mine. And, please, could you tell me which way the angels went?"

"Angels?" said the woman in a startled voice.

She held the crown in her hands, and as she looked at it, long-lost tears ran down her face.

"What is this that is happening to me?" she whispered.

But the little angel had gone—more quickly

now that she had no harp to carry, no crown upon her head. So fast did she go that she almost fell upon a little boy sitting by the roadside and crying as though his heart would break.

"What is that strange sound you are making, little one?" asked the angel.

"I'm crying," the little boy told her. "I wanted to see the King—the new King who is to be in Bethlehem tonight. But they have all gone away and left me. I'm lame, you see, so I can't walk fast, and by the time I get there, the King will be gone."

"A King!" said the angel. "I thought it was a
baby."

"They said he was a King," said the little boy
and he began to cry again.

"Take my wings," said the angel. "You can't

walk very well so it is you who should have them.''

She fastened her wings carefully to his shoulders. They were soft, fluttery things that caught the low night breezes and bore the boy forward in a gentle, rapturous motion.

"Thank you, oh, thank you," he called back, but the little angel scarcely heard him. She was trying to walk without her wings. She had not known it would be so difficult. She kept falling to the ground, and her tender feet were cut and bruised by the stones in the roadway.

"But the big star is there," she thought, as she went slowly along. "And see, a light! Is it Heaven at last?"

But it was not a light from Heaven she saw— only candles from a home nearby.

The angel knocked timidly and stood waiting—
a little thing with pleading eyes and tangled golden
hair.

A woman opened the door, then stood staring at
the little angel, unable to believe what she saw.

"Peter," she whispered back into the room. "Peter, come! Do you see what I see? Oh, is it a miracle because we have prayed so long? Is this a child sent to us at last?"

She put out her hands and drew the lost angel
to her. She bathed the soiled and bleeding feet and
combed the tangled hair. Then she held her close
and sang a low song of great joy, and the little angel
closed her eyes and dreamed that she was in Heaven

When she awoke it was morning. She had found not Heaven but a new home and a mother and father.

They so loved her that she almost forgot she had been a little angel. She ran about the fields while the man Peter tended his sheep, and she helped the

woman Dorcas make the bread and sweep the floor.
She played in the meadows and vineyards with the
other children, and they loved her because she was
so gentle and sweet.

Many years passed, and Peter and Dorcas at last grew old and passed away. But the lost angel stayed in their home alone. Now it was she who tended the sheep and gathered the grapes and made the bread. She was friendly to all who came to her door. Many travellers knocked there and always found a welcome, food, and rest. They told her about the far lands through which they had come and of the people they had met or of whom they had heard.

Many of their stories were of the great ones in the world. They told her of a poet who sang his way straight into the hearts of men. They told of a greathearted woman who spent her life helping the poor and the sinful. They told her of a leader of the people—lame, it is true, but inspired and beloved.